An I Can Read Book®

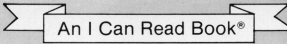

A GHOST NAMED FRED

by NATHANIEL BENCHLEY

Pictures by BEN SHECTER

HarperCollins*Publishers*

This book is a presentation of Atlas Editions, Inc.
For information about Atlas Editions book clubs write to:
Atlas Editions, Inc.
4343 Equity Drive, Columbus, Ohio 43228

Published by arrangement with HarperCollins Publishers.

1998 edition

A GHOST NAMED FRED
Text copyright © 1968 by Nathaniel G. Benchley
Pictures copyright © 1968 by Ben Shecter

Library of Congress Catalog Card Number: 68-24322
ISBN 0-06-020473-7
ISBN 0-06-020474-5 (lib. bdg.)

For Brendan Upson, *the man with the idea*

George had nobody to play with.

The boys who lived near him
were either too old or too young.

So he had to make up his own games.

One day he would be a pirate,

another day a pilot.

In the tub he would be a submarine,

and in bed he was a bear in a cave.

One day George played

he was an astronaut in orbit,

and he got a long way away from home.

It began to get dark,

and he didn't know how to get back.

Then it started to rain.

George saw an old house

in the darkness.

"I guess I had better go there,"

he said.

"If I don't, I'll get my feet wet

and probably catch cold."

So he went to the house and knocked,

but there was no answer.

Just the sound of the rain.

And thunder.

The door was unlocked.

George pushed it and looked inside.

It was dark, but it was also dry.

"I will just go in for a minute,"
George said.

"Until the rain stops."

The house was cold

and smelled of dust and damp.

George felt that something

was coming near him,

but he couldn't see it.

Whatever it was,

he didn't like it.

He went into another room,

but still he felt the thing

coming closer.

It made his skin feel cold,

and his hair began to prickle.

"I think I'll go upstairs,"

he said.

"There is something wrong down here."

He went upstairs,

and just as he reached

the top of the stairs

he heard a *voice* behind him!

It said: "Do you mind telling me
what that is on your head?"

"Who is that?" said George.

"Where are you?"

"Right behind you," said the voice.

"Look here."

George looked and saw two eyes.

"Who are you?"

he asked the eyes.

"Are you a ghost?"

"Yes," the eyes replied.

"But I'd rather have
you call me Fred.

And I still want to know
what is on your head."

"Oh, that," said George.

"I had forgotten about that."

"It's my hat I used

when I was playing astronaut."

"Please take it off," said Fred.

"It makes your voice sound odd."

So George took off the hat.

"Is that better?" he asked.

"Much," Fred replied.

"You have a nice voice,

if you give it a chance."

"Thank you," said George.

"Nobody ever told me that before."

"What brings you here?" asked Fred.

"This is no place for a boy alone."

"I got lost," said George.

"What about you?

Why are you here?"

"It's a long story," Fred replied.

"But to be brief about it,

I am here to guard some treasure."

"Treasure?" George cried.

"Where is it?"

"I wouldn't be much of a guard

if I told you," said Fred.

"I'm going to let you guess."

"Is it in the attic?" George asked.

"No."

"The cellar?"

"No."

"The kitchen?"

"No."

"The bedroom?"

"No."

"Then I give up. Where is it?"

Fred made a little coughing sound.

"To tell the truth, I've forgotten,"

he said.

"I was hoping you would remind me."

"Then let's look," said George.

"You're sure it's in the house?"

"Just about," said Fred.

"I saw it once,

but that was long ago.

Let's try downstairs."

They went downstairs, and

in the pantry they found three mice.

"Have you seen the treasure?"

George asked.

"We're not interested in treasure,"
the mice replied.

"We're looking for cheese."

"You came to the wrong house," said Fred.

"There hasn't been cheese here since the party my mother gave for her aunt."

"Just our luck," said the mice, and they left.

In the library they found

an old bat, hanging upside down.

"Charlie," Fred said to the bat,

"you've been here a long time.

Do you remember where the treasure is?"

"My father knew," said Charlie.

"But he hasn't been seen

since last Hallowe'en.

If he ever comes back, I'll ask him."

"That's no help," said Fred.

"We want to find it now.

Come help us look."

"All right," said Charlie.

"It's time I flew anyway.

If I had hung there much longer,

I would have got a nosebleed."

So the three of them

went all through the house

but saw no sign of the treasure.

In the front hall was a clock,

and George said, "Oh, I'm late!

I must be getting home."

"You had better take an umbrella,"
said Fred.

"There is one in that closet there."
So George took the umbrella
and opened it.

And out poured the treasure!

"That's it!" cried Fred.

"You've found it!"

George counted out the treasure,
and Fred let him take one coin home

as a souvenir.

But on thinking it over,

George decided

he wouldn't show it to anyone.

He just kept it in his pocket

as his secret.